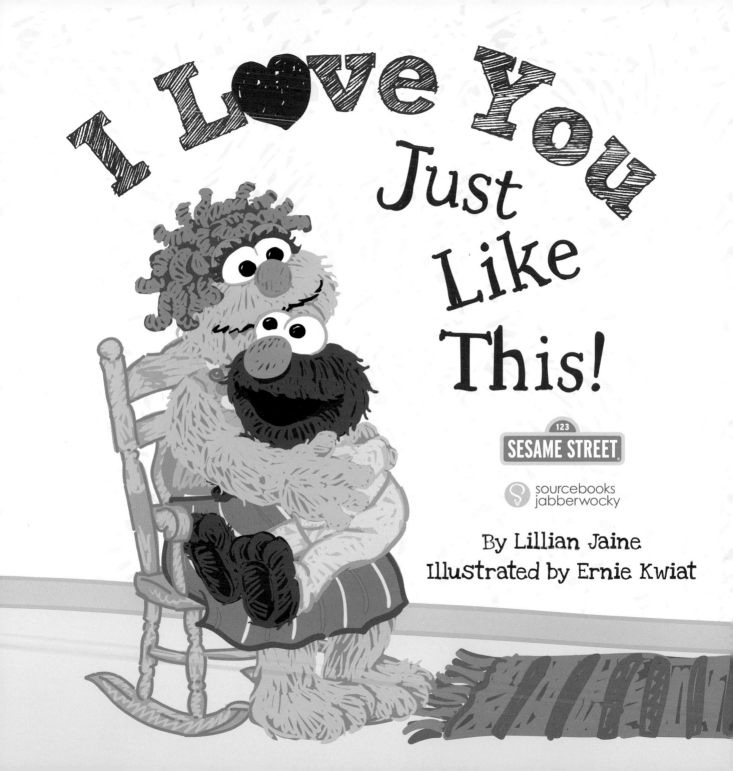

I Love You Just Like This!

123 SESAME STREET

sourcebooks jabberwocky

By Lillian Jaine
Illustrated by Ernie Kwiat

Elmo and his mommy
were talking late one night,
snuggled up together,
cozy, warm, and tight.

"I love you, Mommy,"
Elmo whispered in her ear.
Elmo's mommy smiled.
"I love you too, my dear."

"I've loved you all your life,
every single day.
I love you oh so much—
I'll tell you all the ways!"

I love you brighter
than **1** sun up in the sky.

I love you sweeter than **3** crunchy, yummy treats.

I love you spookier than **5** big flying bats.

I love you taller
than **6** tall, towering hats.

I love you more than the number **7**, **8**, or **9**.

I love you more than **1** through **10** combined!

I love you from your **head**
all the way down to your **toes**.

I love your silly **laugh**,
your **smile**,
and your **nose**.

I love you **redder** than the nicest, reddest rose.

I love you **bluer** than Cookie Monster's toes!

I'd love you if you were **big**

or very, very small.

I'd love you if you were **short**
or really, really **tall**!

I love you when you're **grouchy**
(and even more when you are **sweet**).

I love you when you're ===FAST
or even when you're slow.

I love you **higher** than a hero in the sky.

I love you **deeper**
than the river
rushing by.

I always love you
on a bright and **sunny** day.

I also love you
when the **rain** won't go away.

I love to be with you through
seasons one and all.

I love you all the flowers of **spring** and all the leaves of **fall**.

ve you when you're **near**;
I love you when you're **far**.

I love you **all the time**,
no matter where you are!

I love you often, always,
and time and time again.
I love you from the beginning
to the very end.

Now I'll give you a hug,
and you give me a kiss.
And don't ever forget,

I love you
just like this.

Cover and internal design © 2014 by Sourcebooks, Inc.
Cover illustrations © Sesame Workshop
Text by Lillian Jaine
Illustrations by Ernie Kwiat

Sourcebooks and the colophon are registered trademarks of Sourcebooks, Inc.

Published by Sourcebooks Jabberwocky, an imprint of Sourcebooks, Inc.
P.O. Box 4410, Naperville, Illinois 60567-4410
(630) 961-3900
Fax: (630) 961-2168
www.jabberwockykids.com

Library of Congress Cataloging-in-Publication data is on file with the publisher.

Source of Production: Worzalla, Stevens Point WI, USA
Date of Production: February 2015
Run Number: 5003400

Printed and bound in the United States of America.
WOZ 10 9 8 7 6 5 4 3